THE 22 COMMANDMENTS
All You Will Ever Need to Know About God

A UNIVERSAL MORAL COMPASS
For All People, For All Religions, and For All TIme

FAN MAIL
FANS@SharonEstherLampert.com

"I was reading your 22 Commandments.
Reminds me of a book I recently read by
Rabbi Donniel, "Putting God Second."
In defense from God Intoxication we must
even hold religion accountable to basic
ethical principles."
—Robert

THE 22 COMMANDMENTS

All You Will Ever Need to Know About God

A Universal Moral Compass For All People, For All Religions, and For All Time

KADIMAH PRESS: GIFTS OF GENIUS

Books may be purchased for education, business, or sales promotional use.

ISBN: Hardcover 978-1-885872-03-6
ISBN: Paperback 978-1-885872-04-3
ISBN: E-Book   978-1-885872-05-0
PCN: Library of Congress Control Number: 2008910659

Palm Beach Book Publisher
Full Service: Write, Edit, Publish, Market, Sales
Website: PalmBeachBookPublisher.com
E-mail: Sharon@PalmBeachBookPublisher.com
Phone: 917-767-5843

FAN MAIL:
FANS@SharonEstherLampert.com

WEBSITES:
SharonEstherLampert.com
PhilosopherQueen.com
WorldFamousPoems.com
PoetryJewels.com

Book Design and Interior Creative Genius Sharon Esther Lampert
Editor: Dave Segal

Global Online Websites for Orders and Distribution:
Ingram, 1 Ingram Blvd. La Vergne, TN 37086-3629
Phone: 615-793-5000
Fax orders: 615-287-6990

First Edition

Manufactured in the United States of America

THE 22 COMMANDMENTS
All You Will Ever Need to Know About God

A UNIVERSAL MORAL COMPASS
For All People, For All Religions, and For All TIme

Gift Card

Date:

To:

From:

Message:

GOD IS GO! DO!

God Can Only Do For You What God Can Do Through You!

SHARON ESTHER LAMPERT
KADIMAH: 8TH PROPHETESS OF ISRAEL

THE 22 COMMANDMENTS
All You Will Ever Need to Know About God

A UNIVERSAL MORAL COMPASS
For All People, For All Religions, and For All TIme

KADIMAH PRESS
ISRAEL

What Do Books Do?

BOOKS ARE POWERFUL

Books Educate!
Books Enlighten!
Books Empower!
Books Emancipate!
Books Entertain!
Books Spring Eternal!
Books Drive Exploration!
Books Spark Evolution!
Books Ignite Revolution!

Sharon Esther Lampert

GOD IS GO! DO!

God Can Only Do For You What God Can Do Through You!

Sharon Esther Lampert
PRINCESS KADIMAH: 8TH PROPHETESS OF ISRAEL

KADIMAISM
PhilosopherQueen.com

KADIMAH PRESS: GIFTS OF GENIUS

- Who Knew God Was Such a Chatterbox — God Talks to Me: A Working Definition of God, **GOD IS GO! DO!**

- Unleash the Creator the God Within: 10 Esoteric Laws of Genius and Creativity

- The 22 Commandments: All You Will Ever Need to Know About God

- God of What? 11 Esoteric Laws of Inextricability — Is Life a Gift or a Punishment?

Jews are less than 1% of the human population but 22% of the 5 Nobel Prizes. ISRAEL has 13 Nobel Prizes.

Western Wailing Wall, Jerusalem, Israel

Biographical Note, Age 16

As is the tradition, I left a handwritten note —addressed to God — in the crevices of the Western Wailing Wall in Jerusalem.

It was my first trip to Israel with my parents, on the occasion of my brother Benjamin's Bar Mitzvah that we celebrated at the Western Wall.

I visited my first cousins Bunya and Yankle Lampert and their sons, my second cousins Israel and Georah Lampert in Ramat Gan, Israel.

I spent four summers in Israel — including a semester at Hebrew University — and one summer at Aish Hatorah having won the award, The Jerusalem Fellowship.

Historical Notes:

Construction started: 19 BC   Height: 62   Length: 488 metres (1,601 ft)

The Western Wall (Kotel Ha'Maarav) is not an actual wall of the Second Temple, it is a retaining wall to the outer courtyard near the Temple built many years after the Temple.

1. The construction of the Western Wall itself was started as part of King Herod's renovations of the Temple Mount that began in the 1st century BCE.

2. After the destruction of the Second Temple in 70 CE, all four of the retaining walls survived.

3. The proximity to the Holy of Holies, the Western Wall became a place of yearning, mourning, and tears for the Jewish people.

4. Jewish law dictates that Jews should pray facing the Kotel, no matter where they are in the world, and this is why Jews face EAST (Kitzur Shulchan Aruch 18:10).

Dedication

Age 16
The Note I Left in the Wailing Wall in Israel

Dear **G**od,
I am not asking for help.
I am offering to be of help.
I am at your service!

Sharon Esther Lampert

Prophet, **P**hilosopher, **P**oet, **P**eacemaker, **P**HOTON SUPERHERO, **P**rodigy

PRINCESS KADIMAH 8TH PROPHETESS OF ISRAEL

EXODUS 31:1-3

1. And the Lord spoke unto Moses, saying,

2. See, I have called by name **BEZALEL** the son of Uri, the son of Hur, of the tribe of Judah:

3. And I have filled him with the spirit of God, in wisdom, and in understanding, and in knowledge, and in all manner of workmanship.

My father Abraham Lampert's nickname was
BEZALEL

"In the Shadow of God" the Architect who built the Ark of the Covenant, **EXODUS 31:1-3**

I inherited the blessing! — Sharon Esther Lampert

In 1948, my father Abraham Lampert was imprisoned in a Cyprus internment camp for two years, before immigrating to Israel on the boat, AF AL PI CHEN ("In Spite of Everything") Haifa Museum, Israel. Prime Minister Golda Meir visited the camp — He did not ask her for an autograph. My father made these Shabbat candlesticks out of Cyprus stone. The NYC Museum of Jewish Heritage honored him with an exhibit.

(2 Holocaust Video Testimonies: Steven Speilberg Foundation and Museum of Jewish Heritage, NYC)

"How Wonderful it is That
No One Need Wait a Single Minute
Before Starting to Improve the World."

—Anne Frank

WRITER
"Diary of Anne Frank"
One of the 6 Million Jews
Murdered in the Holocaust.
June 12, 1929 – Early March 1945

"Trust Yourself!
Create the kind of self
that you will be happy
to live with all your life.
Make the most of yourself
by fanning the tiny, **inner
sparks** of possibility into
flames of achievement."

—Golda Meir

Fourth Prime Minister of Israel: 1969-1974

May 3, 1898, Kyiv, Ukraine — December 8, 1978, Jerusalem

"Find the Light
and Live in the Light!"

Princess Kadimah: 8TH Prophetess of Israel

Table of Contents

Moses Has 10 Commandments
You Have 22 Commandments
YOU HAD TO OUTDO MOSES!

—Joel Rappelfeld
Ardent Fan, 2002

THE 22 COMMANDMENTS

LIFE
Over Death

STRENGTH
Over Weakness

DEED
Over Sin

LOVE
Over Hatred

TRUTH
Over Lie

COURAGE
Over Fear

OPTIMISM
Over Pessimism

SHARING
Over Selfishness

PRAISE
Over Criticism

LOYALTY
Over Abandonment

RESPONSIBILITY
Over Blame

GRATITUDE
Over Grievances

REWARD
Over Punishment

DEMOCRACY
Over Domination

CREATION
Over Destruction

EDUCATION
Over Ignorance

COOPERATION
Over Competition

FREEDOM
Over Oppression

COMPASSION
Over Indifference

FORGIVENESS
Over Revenge

PEACE
Over War

JOY
Over Suffering

LIFE Over Death
1st Commandment

Q. Is life a gift or a punishment? Measure the pain? Measure the pleasure?

Life is "Temporary Insanity" Here Today — Gone Tommorow!

- We are conceived without our consent or consideration.
- If given a choice — most of us would not agree to be born — life ends in naught!
- We don't have any conscious control over when we are born.
- We do have conscious control over ending our life by suicide.

Make Life Make Sense — Use Letter S:

Part 1. 24/7 Game of Survival from Sunrise to Sunset

Part 2. Socialization: Savage to a Scholar

Part 3. School: Students, Subjects, Study & Study Skills and Skill Set

Part 4. Service to Society and Slavery: Specialists, Schedules, Salary & Status

Part 5. Struggle & Stress, Setbacks & Stumbles, Sacrifices & Suffering

Part 6. Success: Achieved After Struggle, Stress, Sacrifice, and Suffering

Part 7. Society of Saints & Sinners: Smart, Stupid, and Sick

Part 8. Supplication with Scripture, Sermons & Songs to a Savior for SALVATION!

Part 9. Sleep: "Sleep feels as if I'm practicing being dead!" Prophet SEL

Part 10. Sickness, Senility, Strokes, Sorrow, Sadness, Suffering, and Sand Trap!

Part 11. SEX Starts Sequence from Stratch: Survival to Sand Trap

Part 12. Surrender to System: Survival to Sand Trap

STRENGTH Over Weakness
2nd Commandment

Q. Do your strengths overpower your weaknesses or do your weaknesses overpower your strengths?

Nature: When you are born, your genetics determine a great deal of who you are — and what you will be able to do in life. Every person has no other choice but to play the cards they are dealt in life.

Nurture: We have free will to transform weaknesses into strengths.

- Genetics: Play the Cards You are Dealt in Life
- Nature: Always Play to Your Strengths
- Nurture: Transform Weakness into Strength

Strengths over weaknesses: Writing is a creative-right brain and editorial-left brain artistic endeavor. I was born with the gift of creative genius. My creative-right brain writes a poem. My editorial-left brain has to find the irrational typo. I trained my editorial-left brain to find irrational typos. After many years of hard work, my editorial-left brain is now a **strength** — not a weakness!

Destiny: What you do with the cards you are dealt in life determines your destiny!

DEED Over Sin
3rd Commandment

Q. Can you live a moral life in an immoral world?

"You Can Do It All Right and Get It All Wrong!
You Can Do It All Wrong and Get It All Right!"
—Prophet Sharon Esther Lampert

In an immoral world, **GOOD** and **EVIL** have **8** unpredictable outcomes:

Option 1. Good can lead to a greater good
Option 2. Good can lead to good and evil
Option 3. Good can lead to evil
Option 4. Good can lead to nothing
Option 5. Evil can lead to a greater evil
Option 6. Evil can lead to good and evil
Option 7. Evil can lead to a greater good
Option 8. Evil can lead to nothing

MALALA: Evil Leads to a Greater Good

When Malala was shot in the head by a Taliban terrorist in Pakistan,
she was airlifted to the United Kingdom:
- Malala earned a first-rate education in the United Kingdom.
- Malala was honored with a Nobel Prize.
- Malala raises money to educate women in 3rd-world countries.

MARTHA SMART: Good Leads to Evil Leads to a Greater Good

Martha Smart's father gave a homeless man a job. The homeless man
abducted his daughter and raped her every day for nine months.
    Martha Smart became an advocate on behalf of abducted children.

An old Jewish joke:
Three Jewish mothers are sitting on a bench, arguing over which one's son loves her the most. The first one says, "You know, my son sends me flowers every Shabbos." "You call that love?" says the second mother. "My son calls me every day!" "That's nothing," says the third woman. "My son is in therapy five days a week. And the whole time, he talks about me!"

LOVE Over Hatred
4th Commandment

"All people **help you** with their strengths and **hurt you** with their weaknesses!"
—Prophet Sharon Esther Lampert

Q. What is LOVE?

Q. Why is the person you love and married the same person you hate and divorced?

"You Don't Find Love, You Create Love"
—Prophet Sharon Esther Lampert

What is **LOVE?** Respect, Understanding, Empathy, Kindness, and Tolerance.

1. **TRUE LOVE** is unconditional love. Unconditional love is real... but rare!
2. **Happliy Married Couples Married Their Best Friends!**
3. SELF: The most important relationship is the one you have with yourself:
   - Be Your Own Best Friend!
   - Self-Care is Not Selfish!
   - Self-Love is True Love!
   - Love from Outside Yourself Is **BONUS LOVE!**

"There is No Such Thing as Too Much **Love**!"
—Prophet Sharon Esther Lampert

4. OTHER: You can never know another person!
   - You marry, have sex and children with a stranger and divorce a stranger.
   - Most love is conditional love — a give and take transaction for services rendered.
   - Some people love only what they want from you.
   - Some people do not have the capacity to love: 100% SELFISH!
   - Some people do not have the capacity to love themselves or you!
   - The divorce rate is HIGH because couples disrespect each other, and treat each other like disposables — as if they are throwing away the trash!

TRUTH Over Lie
5th Commandment

Q. Is honesty always the best policy?

"THERE IS ONLY ONE
TRUTH
NO ONE HAS THE TRUTH"
—Prophet Sharon Esther Lampert

Transform Information into Knowledge and Knowledge into Wisdom
—Prophet Sharon Esther Lampert

- Truth & lie are complex variables in a compound equation of opinions, belief systems, and facts.
- People lie because they are taught lies instead of the truth.
- People lie because they cannot distinguish fact from fiction.
- Only tell the truth to people you trust — your enemies will betray you!
- Facts are updated to reflect our current understanding of the world.

As an Academic Intervention Specialist, parents often complain that their kids lie to them about schoolwork. These kids do not have study skills to achieve academic success. Lying and cheating are acts of survival in a malfunctioning education system. Educators do not know how to cultivate the awesome power of the human brain! Lying and cheating to survive school — and an antiquated education system is fomented in the first grade.

COURAGE Over Fear
6th Commandment

Q. Are you able to overcome your fears,
or do you surrender to your fears?

"Courage is the most important of all the virtues,
because without courage you can't practice any other
virtue consistently. You can practice any virtue erratically,
but nothing consistently without courage"
— Poet Maya Angelou

Plan in Place on Paper: Plan A, Plan B, Plan C, Plan C, Plan D

You start the day on **Plan A** — but you end the day on **Plan D**.
Each day, you are beset with an obstacle course of unforeseen
obstacles — delays, detours, disappointments, and distractions.
At each juncture, you must summon the COURAGE to overcome
the obstacle course to achieve your daily objectives.

Success is not a straight line — it is a roller-coaster ride
of highs and lows beset with stress, struggle, and sacrifice.

How do you summon the COURAGE day in and day out?
One day at a time and one foot in front of the other.
Celebrate every day! Eat a nutritious breakfast to begin the day
with the energy to endure each day's adventures of highs and lows.
Listen to inspirational music — the greatest joy in the world!

An old Jewish joke:
What's the difference between a pessimist and an optimist?
The pessimist says, "It can't possibly get any worse than this."
The optimist says, "Of course it can!"

OPTIMISM Over Pessimism
7th Commandment

Q. Is your glass half empty or half full?

"ALL YOU GET FOR NEGATIVITY IS NOTHING"
—Prophet Sharon Esther Lampert

When You FREE Your Mind of Negativity, 10 MIRACLES HAPPEN!

Miracle 1. Inner Critic: Stop beating up on yourself!

Miracle 2. Inner Enemy: Stop getting in your own way!

Miracle 3. Stop comparing yourself to others - you play the cards you are dealt!

Miracle 4. Unconditionally love yourself. SELF-CARE IS NOT SELFISH!

Miracle 5. Family is talking to you because you stopped finding fault with them!

Miracle 6. Make friends instead of enemies!

Miracle 7. Life your best life!

Miracle 8. Heal from pain of the past: Tragedy, Trauma, Triumph!

Miracle 9. Stop complaining about what's wrong with the world!

Refocus your attention on what is right with the world!

Miracle 10. You cannot right the wrongs of the past — each day is a fresh start!

SHARING Over Selfishness
8th Commandment

Q. Do you prefer to give more than what's expected of you — and run the extra mile, or do you prefer to cut corners, and give less than your share or nothing at all?

We Learn to Share
Sharing is a Virtue — Practice Sharing

We are taught to give before we take.

Before the age of two, one of the first life lessons in life is learning to share your toys with siblings. In school, you will learn to share your crayons with fellow students.

There are vast gender differences between what a woman is expected to give to her family — and what a man is expected to give to his work, occupation, and profession.

There are religious laws that enforce giving charity to the needy.

There are government laws that encourage tax deductions if you give charity to a worthy non-profit cause.

There are student- loan programs that encourage giving your time to help others to earn tuition-reduction credits.

Giving and taking are complex variables. Some give time, some give money, and some give material things to help others.

We give and take differently.

An old Jewish joke: A group of five Jewish women are eating lunch in a busy cafe. Nervously, their waiter approaches the table. "Ladies," he says. "Is anything okay?"

PRAISE Over Criticism
9th Commandment

Q. Do you prefer to find something nice to say, or do you prefer to look for faults, lash out, and criticize, and become judge, jury, and executioner?

- **Praise** Is Pleasure.
- **Criticism** Is Pain.
- **Constructive Criticism**: First Pain — Then Pleasure

When a crawling child learns how to talk and walk, parents do not criticize the child when the child falls down — they continuously encourage,

"You Can Do It!   Great Job!   I Love You!"

In my role as an **Academic Learning Specialist**, the very first step is to rebuild a child's self-esteem. It was destroyed by a blizzard of criticisms, such as, "lazy, stupid, and ADHD" by parents, teachers, and psychiatrists. The student is living in a war zone of criticism!

Parents have a system of punishments that humiliate the child. Parents are breaking down the child — not building the child up!

Once children shut down — they tune out the parent, teachers, and psychiatrists! The child is stressed and depressed! **"I don't care!"** is the child's clarion call.

LOYALTY Over Abandonment
10th Commandment

Q. Do you show support to family and friends during difficult times, or do you run in the opposite direction and "ghost" your family, relatives, and friends?

Loyalty Is a Virtue
Practice Loyalty

Right after college, my mother passed away after a 6-year brutal battle with breast cancer. After a 6-year battle, my family was exhausted from the fight.

I am the firstborn, so like other firstborns, we are born and bred to take command of the ship and steer it into safe waters. There was no instruction manual to navigate the treacherous terrain when the family matriarch had fallen in defeat at age 59.

During difficult times, family ties break apart, friends run for the hills — and one is left alone to endure the devastation.

The opposite is also true!

Families close ranks, come together, become closer, and are always there for each other with helping hands and loving hearts.

RESPONSIBILITY Over Blame
11th Commandment

Q. Do you blame and scapegoat others instead of taking responsibility and solving the problem?

Responsibility Is a Virtue
Practice Responsibility

The **BLAME GAME** resolves nothing — it is a futile endeavor. We have to learn how to work together to solve problems. Problem-solving is a learned skill.

Every problem is a complex equation of compound variables.
It takes years — or centuries— to understand complex problems:
- In medicine, we have to find the cure for cancer.
- In politics, we have to keep guns out of the hands of the mentally ill.
- In science, we have to find ways to solve the climate crisis.

My focus is on solving the **National Education Crisis**!
- Teachers blame parents — a futile endeavor.
- Parents blame teachers — a futile endeavor.

My book, "The Silent Crisis Destroying America's Brightest Minds." deftly elucidates the problem and the solution to the problem. Parents now have resources to help their kids achieve academic success in school.

GRATITUDE Over Greivances
12th Commandment

- -

Q. Do you count your blessings
　 or do you count your curses?

- -

Gratitude Is a Virtue
Practice Gratitude

Gratitude means taking stock of all of life's blessings.
Start by making a list of your blessings.
Each day, read your list of blessings:
- I am alive
- I am healthy
- I have food in my belly
- I have clothes on my back
- I have an education

Gratitude is a daily practice:
- Gratitude decreases anxiety.
- Gratitude decreases stress.
- Gratitude decreases bouts of depression.

There is an exponential relationship between HAPPINESS and GRATITUDE.

More Gratitude = More Happiness!

REWARD Over Punishment
13th Commandment

Q. When do you punish? When do you reward?

Rewards are used to encourage or discourage behavior.
Punishments are used to encourage or discourage behavior.
Rewards are positive reinforcement.
Punishments are negative reinforcement.

In psychology, this area of study is called Behaviorism.
Operant conditioning states that when a behavior is
rewarded, it encourages us to repeat the behavior.
When behavior is punished, we are discouraged from repeating the behavior.

Do you want to encourage or discourage the behavior?
When we err, we need to learn how to self-correct.
Neither rewards or punishments help us build new skills.

I prefer a system of rewards because children feel good when
earning rewards. When children are punished, they feel humiliated
for making mistakes — punishments take a toll on self-esteem —
and erodes confidence.

Children Cannot Raise Themselves — It is Never the Child's Fault!

All Children Want to Succeed! — They Just Don't Know How!

DEMOCRACY Over Domination
(MERITOCRACY Over Democracy)
14th Commandment

Q. How can we cultivate a world that allows all voices to be heard, respected, and validated?

We are all born into authoritarian **BIRTH BUBBLES!**

In family dynamics, parents make 100% of the decisions for a child — until a child speaks out, and voices an opinion. At first, when a child speaks out — he is rebellious! For example, a child may no longer want to eat the same food as the rest of the family — or may no longer want to practice the same religion.

We begin our lives on a default setting — later, we live our lives by design. The development of one's inner voice is a lifelong journey. Everyone has an inner GPS that determines one's unique destiny!

Democracy is flourishing in many parts of the world. People prefer to cast a **VOTE** as to who will lead their country.

Democracy works if educated people make intelligent decisions based on merit — not popularity. Too often, people are misinformed. Too often, politicians lack professional experience. Too often, popular yet unqualified politicians win.

DEMOCRACY takes into account every voice — but in the end — not every voice will be heard. Only the voices who won the election will be heard.

MERITOCRACY is a better system than democracy: Mayors run for governor; Governors run for congress; Congressmen run for president — just like in every other profession — you earn the right to advance based on achievement.

CREATION Over Destruction
15th Commandment

Q. Can you throw an empty glass on the floor, and destroy it into hundreds of broken shards? Yes! How many can create a glass to drink water?

There are Two Kinds of Men in the World:
BIG DICKS Who Know How to Build Something, and
SMALL DICKS Who Know How to Destroy Everything!

—Prophet Sharon Esther Lampert

Nature: We are born ignorant, irrational, unconscious, and destructive — even a toddler can throw a glass on the floor and break it!

Nurture: To become creators, we need an education:

We are hungry — We have to plant seeds to reap our harvest.

We are thirsty — We have to purify water to quench our thirst.

We are naked — We have to weave yarn to sew our clothing.

We are cold — We have to build a roof over our heads.

We are sleepy — We have to build a bed for a goodnight's sleep.

We are afraid of each other — We have to learn how to love.

We are interdependent — We need to learn how to collaborate.

We are ignorant — We have to go to school and study.

EDUCATION Over Ignorance
16th Commandment

Q. Is ignorance bitter or bliss?

THERE IS ONE GLOBAL ENEMY
IGNORANCE!

"What if we could solve just one problem in the world, and by solving that one problem — we could solve every problem in the world?

If We Just Solve The

PROBLEM OF EDUCATION

We Will Be Able to Solve Every Problem in The World

PHOTON SUPERHERO OF EDUCATION
SMARTGRADES: BRAIN POWER REVOLUTION
www.smartgrades.com

COOPERATION Over Competition
17th Commandment

Q. Are we able to work together to achieve goals?

We are interdependent — no one can survive without the concerted efforts of millions of people around the world.

Collaboration is a required essential skill to maintain our civilization. Collaboration is a **WIN:WIN** game plan.

When we compete with each other, we create a **WIN: LOSE** game plan. Someone has to **WIN** and someone has to **LOSE**.

What game plan are you on? There are three games in life:

- **WIN: WIN   e.g., ORCHESTRA**
- **WIN: LOSE   e.g., SPORTS**
- **LOSE: LOSE e.g., WAR**

How Can We Redesign Every Game for a WIN: WIN! ?
e.g., An orchestra is an extraordinary collaboration of musicians.

e.g., Moviemaking is a masterful collaboration of artistic talents:
- Being cast in a movie is a **WIN!**
- Being a working actor with a paycheck is a **WIN!**
- Receiving an Oscar nomination is a **WIN!**
- During the Oscar's, each movie nominated **WINS** an award for a contribution to moviemaking, e.g., costumes or cinematography.

FREEDOM Over Oppression
18th Commandment

- -

Q.   How to we liberate people from oppression in all
of its forms: racism, sexism, illiteracy, and poverty.

- -

"I ask no favor for my sex.
All I ask of our brethren is that
they take their feet off our necks."

—Justice Ruth Bader Ginsburg arguing before the
U.S. Supreme Court, quoting abolitionist Sarah Grimké

I was blessed to be raised in a Jewish egalitarian community — The Jewish
Theological Seminary of America — where men and women were treated as equals.
Moreso, if women were smarter — men handed over the reins to the women.

During my lifetime, I experienced the oppression of sexist microaggressions,

"Did you write this poem all by yourself?"

As a consequence of the **DIGITAL REVOLUTION**, we can all see each other
in the online universe of the internet.
- We are all talking to each other — and sharing our recipes.
- We are globally connected and invested in each other's lives.
- As a global community, we value freedom for all peoples.

COMPASSION Over Indifference
19th Commandment

Q. Do you practice compassion or indifference?

Compassion Is a Virtue
Practice Compassion

Radical empathy is the ability to see the world from the point of view of another person.

It is impossible to walk in another person's shoes — but it is not impossible to learn how to listen to someone else's life story and practice compassion.

We live in alternative universes with different values, priorities, and goals. There are many interesting options as to how to live one's life:
- One person wants to be married and have a big family.
- Another person wants to live alone — without people, plants, or pets.
- One person lives in an urban jungle.
- Another person lives in a rural town far way from civilization.

Most of us choose sides: We care about some people — and are indifferent to people who do not comply with our way of life.

- Practice the art of compassion in every conversation.
- Don't judge others by your life experiences!

"What an interesting life story... tell me more!"

FORGIVENESS Over Revenge
20th Commandment

- -

Q. Are you quick or slow to forgive yourself, family, and
friends when they make mistakes?

Q. Do you want to make amends or take revenge?

- -

Forgiveness Is a Virtue
Practice Forgiveness

Five Options:
Option 1.　Forgive and Forget!
Option 2.　Forgive but Never Forget!
Option 3.　Never Forgive and Never Forget!
Option 4.　Seek Retribution and Revenge!
Option 5.　Never Forgive, Never Forget, Seek Retribution, Revenge,
　　　　　　and Compensation!

All people have strengths and weaknesses. Without exception—
everyone makes mistakes! Some mistakes are inconsequential.
Some mistakes result in unspeakable tragedy. This is not black and
white — only shades of grey. Our society of saints and sinners is a
composite of Smart%, Stupid% and Sick%
Personally, I prefer to choose Option 2.
"Living Well is the Best Revenge!" is an adage that speaks to my
heart and soul. I may have become a victim of a cloaked nefarious
psychopath — but I want to be both the Victor & Victorious!

I Cannot Right the Wrongs of the Past! Tomorrow Is a New Day!

> "The human animal talks like a human being — but always behaves like a human animal. **ALL EVIL IS JUSTIFIED!**"
> —Prophet Sharon Lampert

PEACE Over War
21st Commandment

Q. Why is the barbarism of war an option in the 21st century?

"The only place to find **Peace** on **Planet Earth** is in a cemetery."
— Prophet Sharon Esther Lampert

Peace Is A Virtue
Practice Peace

- The world is full of so much hatred — most of it — centuries old!
- Most people do not have to look outside their families to find hatred!
- There is no other animal — except for the human animal — that treats its own species with the malevolent malice of war and genocide!

ALL EVIL IS JUSTIFIED!

Nature: There are 8.7 million living beings on Planet Earth — and they all fear each other, hate each other — and many have to eat each other to survive.

Nurture: Children are taught at a young age to distinguish allies from enemies — especially by race, religion, and politics.

2021: The downfall of a democratic Afghanistan — and the home imprisonment of millions of Afghan women.

2022: Putin's war in Ukraine: 44-million people terrorized! Centuries of hatred! The world's greatest fear is upon us — a madman with nukes!

JOY Over Suffering
22nd Commandment

Q. What is **JOY**?

Q. Can you add more **JOY** to your life ?

Joy Is A Virtue
Practice Joy

What is JOY? JOY is happiness, fulfillment, and pleasure.

Make a list of what makes you happy, gives you pleasure, and fulfillment, and brings you JOY!

As a child, I kept a list of all of my favorite things that made me happy. Even on a bad day, I could check my list —and make sure that every day of my life has a happy component.

Here is my list of what brings me JOY!
- My MOMMY
- My Two Cats: Schmaltzy & Falafel, schmaltzy.com
- My APPLE Computer
- My Sports, Music, Books, and Beach!
- Chocolate
- NYC Night Life: Broadway Shows, Concerts, Opera

The 8 Prophetesses of Israel

Sarah
Ageless Beauty, Seer, Holy Spirit
- Genesis 17:15-17:27
- Genesis 18:1-18:15
- Genesis 21:1-21:22
- Genesis 23:1-23:20

Miriam
Saved the life of Moses
- Exodus 2:1-2:10
- Exodus 15:20-15:27
- Numbers 12:1-12:16
- Numbers 20:1-20:6

Deborah
Warrior and 4th Judge
- Judges 4:4-4:14
- Judges 5:1-5:31

Hannah
Personal Prayer
- 1 Samuel 1:1-1:28

Abigail
Prophecy of King David
- 1 Samuel 25:2-25:44
- 1 Samuel 27:1-27:3
- 1 Samuel 30:4
- 2 Samuel 2:2
- 2 Samuel 3:2

Huldah
Learning, Enlightenment, and Peace
- 2 Kings 22:1-20

Esther
Rescued Jews from Genocide
- Esther 2:7-2:23
- Esther 4:1-4:16
- Esther 5:1-5:8
- Esther 7:1-7:10
- Esther 8:3-8:8
- Esther 9:12-9:14
- Esther 9:26-9:32

Sharon Esther Lampert
- 22 Commandments
- World Peace Equation
- 40 Absolute Truths
- World Poetry Record
- 40 Universal Gold Standards of Education
- 22 Steps to Find a Soulmate
- 10 Thinking Tools of Creative Genius

EXODUS 31:1-3

All You Will Ever Need to Know About God
The 22 Commandments
A Universal Moral Compass For All People, For All Religions, and For All Time

1. LIFE
Over Death

2. STRENGTH
Over Weakness

3. DEED
Over Sin

4. LOVE
Over Hatred

5. TRUTH
Over Lie

6. WISDOM
Over Stupidity

7. OPTIMISM
Over Pessimism

8. SHARING
Over Selfishness

9. PRAISE
Over Criticism

10. LOYALTY
Over Abandonment

11. RESPONSIBILITY
Over Blame

12. GRATITUDE
Over Envy

13. REWARD
Over Punishment

14. DEMOCRACY
Over Domination

15. CREATION
Over Destruction

16. EDUCATION
Over Ignorance

17. COOPERATION
Over Competition

18. FREEDOM
Over Oppression

19. COMPASSION
Over Indifference

20. FORGIVENESS
Over Revenge

21. PEACE
Over War

22. JOY
Over Suffering

"Moses had 10 commandments. You have 22 commandments. You had to out do Moses."
Joel Rapplefeld

"Inside Every Jewish Person Is a Little Moses Tying to Get Out."
Chabad Rabbi Ben Tzion Krasnianski

Sharon Esther Lampert
KADIMAH
8TH Prophetess of Israel

Learn It. Live It. Share it.

---

1. Sarah: (Genesis 21:12)
Ageless Beauty, Seer, Holy Spirit

2. Miriam: Exodus 15:21
Saved the life of Moses

3. Devorah: Judges 4:4
Warrior and 4th Judge

4. Chanah: I Samuel 2:1-10
Personal Prayer

5. Abigail: I Samuel (25:2-44)
Prophecy of King David

6. Huldah: Kings 22:14
Learning, Enlightenment, and Peace

7. Esther: The Book of Esther
Saved the Jews from Genocide

8. Kadimah: 22 Commandments
Beauty, Seer, Holy Spirit, Learning, Enlightenment and World Peace

THE 22 COMMANDMENTS

All You Will Ever Need to Know About God

GOD IS GO! DO!

God Can Only Do For You What God Can Do Through You!

World Religions

Atheism
Atheists are people who believe that god or gods are man-made constructs.

Baha'i
One of the youngest of the world's major religions.

Buddhism
A way of living based on the teachings of Siddhartha Gautama.

Candomblé
A religion based on African beliefs, originating in Brazil.

Christianity
The world's biggest faith, based on the teaching of Jewish Jesus Christ.

Hinduism
A group of faiths rooted in the religious ideas of India.

Islam
Revealed in its final form by the Prophet Muhammad.

Jainism
An ancient philosophy and ethical teaching that originated in India.

Jehovah's Witnesses
A Christian-based evangelistic religious movement.

Judaism
Based around the Jewish people's covenant relationship with God.

KADIMAISM
Based on **THE 22 COMMANDMENTS**, by Sharon Esther Lampert, the 8TH Prophetess of Israel A Universal Moral Compass For All People, For All Religions, and For All Time. **GOD IS GO! DO!** God Can Only Do For You What God Can Do Through You!

Mormonism
The Church of Jesus Christ of Latter-day Saints.

World Religions

Paganism
Contemporary religions usually based on reverence for nature.

Rastafari
A young religion founded in Jamaica in the 1930s.

Santeria
Afro-Caribbean syncretic religion originating in Cuba.

Modern Belief Systems
Secularism; Atheism; Agnosticim; Skepticiam; Humanism; Naturalism;
and Rationalism

Shinto
Japanese folk tradition and ritual with no founder or single sacred scripture.

Sikhism
The religion founded by Guru Nanak in India in the 15th Century CE.

Spiritualism
Spiritualists believe in communication with the spirits of people who have died.

Taoism
An ancient tradition of philosophy and belief rooted in Chinese worldview.

Unitarianism
An open-minded and individualistic approach to religion.

Zoroastrianism
One of the oldest monotheistic faiths, founded by the Prophet Zoroaster.

EPIC POEM
In 5 Minutes
Learn 5000 Years of Jewish History

By Sharon Esther Lampert - In Celebration of 50TH Birthday

Many Jews Reclaimed God

By Divine Words and Divine Works, Abraham and Sarah, Isaac and Rebecca, Jacob, Leah, and Rachel conceived a holy people. Familiar family faith. In an ark, Noah was not consumed; a rainbow ascended. Adam blamed Eve, and the Garden of Eden was left behind. Joseph cast into a pit and prison, was recast as a prince of Egypt. The silver goblet ascended. Benjamin was not left behind. Familiar family forgiveness. Divine convenants of spiritual and physical dimensions were contracted with Abraham, Noah, Jacob, and Moses. Seven prophetesses ascended: Sarah, Miriam, Deborah, Hannah, Abigail, Huldah and Esther; the first beauty queen contestant. All Hebrews became physically and spiritually enslaved in Egypt; mortar descended and bricks ascended. GOD spoke to Moses and Moses once-and-once-again received The Ten Commandments. The burning bush was not consumed. Twelve tribes ascended. All of the Children of Israel received The **Ten Commandments** in the barren desert. Many Jews became spiritually liberated.

MANY JEWS FOUND GOD

All Jews wanted physical deliverance from the barren desert. Many Jews found the homeland and became Israelites, a miracle. Moses was left behind. All Jews were divided into two kingdoms: Northern Kingdom of Israel in Samaria and Southern Davidic Kingdom of Judah in Judea. Some Jews remained Jews after the Assyrian exile, Babylonian exile, and destruction of the First Temple. Some Jews remained Jews after the Roman exile and destruction of the Second Temple. King Saul, King David, and King Solomon ascended. Ascending and descending, messiahs, miracles, and martyrs were left behind. All Canaanite, Philistine, Ammonite, Moabite, Midianite, Sumerian, Assyrian, Hittite, Babylonian, Persian, and Roman Empires, and ALL of their **GODS** were left behind. Dream of Zion renewed was not left behind. All Jews underwent the wear and tear of conquest, destruction, and exile.

SOME JEWS HAD FORSAKEN GOD

Exiled from their homeland, all Jews prayed for spiritual redemption from the religious oppression of the Diaspora. All Jews who remained Jews found incessant forced conversions, persecutions, and pogroms throughout Western and Eastern Europe. Thirty-four expulsions were recorded: For 2000 years, Christian hatred of the Jews consumed. Many Jews died "Al Kiddush Hashem." Thousands upon thousands of Christians fought against the enemies of Christ. Thousands upon thousands of Muslims fought against the infidels: Christians vs. Muslims (to this very day) each take turns leaving each other behind...proselytes vs. apostates. **The Greatest Lie Ever Told in the Name of GOD** descended: The death of Jesus was good for Christians and bad for Jews. For Christians: **"Jesus Died for You, So You Can Live and You Get Eternal Life."** For Jews: **"Jesus Died and You Killed Him and You Get Premature Death."** Relationships of religion, resources, and revenue were familiar family lies. Many Jews witnessed verbal slanders turned into violent physical deeds.

ALL JEWS SAW THEIR FATE IN GOD'S HANDS

All Jews and only Jews were no longer given choices: economic discrimination, social ostracism, personal humiliation, and the **"THE FINAL SOLUTION."** Familiar family lies. The yellow star descended. Jews, cast as wandering exiles, were recast for genocide. Swastikas descended. Less than one fourth of one percent of the world's population were targeted for extermination. Shaved heads and tatooed numbers burned into arms descended. Many Jews were deported to concentration camps (human flesh burning crematoria, gas chambers, and hospital rooms for scientific experimentation): Zyklon-B gas was consumed. One third of worldwide Jewry was annilated. Six million sacred Jewish souls were left behind, their physical bodies exterminated, their seeds of immortality extinguished. A few Jews committed suicide on their way to, inside of, and soon after, the ominous death camps.

SOME JEWS LOST GOD

Homebound, all Jews wanted to go home. Some Jews had families and some Jews were orphans. All Jews were the children of God. Ascending, some Jews went to Canada; a few Jews went to South Africa where the world was divided into white on black; a few Jews went to Argentina with the escaped Nazis. The Jewish Brigade of Palestine was not consumed. The slogan, **"Jews Can Fight and Jews Can Win"** ascended. In the Pope's office, blaming the Jews for **DEICIDE** was left behind. UN Resolution 3379, Zionism was Racism, was left behind. Many Jews went to America with ALL worldwide refugees (to this very day). On the Statue of Liberty, Emma Lazarus's poetry ascended. Irving Berlin's compositions, "God Bless America" and "Israel" ascended. Ascending, the sexiest woman alive, Marilyn Monroe, converted to Judaism. In Sweden, Alfred Nobel, cast as a dynamite manufacturer, was recast as the good will manufacturer of Nobel Prizes. Jewish genius ascended and was recognized : For WORLD PEACE: Alfred H. Fried (1911); ... For ECONOMICS: Paul A. Samuelson (1970); ... For CHEMISTRY: Adolph Von Baeyer (1905);... For PHYSICS: Albert Abraham Michaelson (1907);... For MEDICINE and PHYSIOLOGY: Elie Metchnikoff (1908); ... Jews hold 22% of the Nobel Prizes. Jews wrote the popular Christmas songs: White Christmas, Rudolph, The Red-Nosed Reindeer, Let it Snow, Silver Bells, and Chestnuts Roasting on the Open Fire. Ascending, worldwide, humanity as a whole benefits from these magnificent, monumental, and momentous contributions from less than one fourth of one percent of the world's population. In 50 countries, Lubavitch-Chabad emissaries were left behind and not consumed: Jewish spiritual reinvigoration ascended. Many Jews witnessed a glimmer of the glorious face of **GOD**.

SOME JEWS SAW GOD EVERYWHERE

HOME SWEET HOME: Jews from every country in the world went home: Jews from 102 countries, speaking 82 languages ascended. On May 14, 1948, the vision of Theodor Herzl ascended: First as pioneers, then as soldiers and citizens, and finally as Zionists. The national anthem, **"Hatikvah,"** ascended. The Hebrew language ascended. Falafel in pita with tehina sauce was consumed. A miracle: "The Old Israel's" GOD YHWH was not consumed in the Holocaust. Triumphant, the Israel Defense Forces ascended. All Jews, cast as sacrificial lambs, were recast as sacrificial LIONS: Arab Riots and Revolts, War of Independence, Suez Canal, Six-Day War, Yom Kippur War, Lebanon War, Iraqi Scud Missile Crisis, and Incessant Terrorism descended. The Nation of Israel reborn was reckoned with, reconciled with, and was recognized by the world. Israeli operations resettled the exiles and unsettled the enemies. In this birthplace of ancient miracles, modern miracles of medicine, science, and technology ascended. Democracy ascended. Haredi, Dati, Masorti, Hiloni ascended, Women of the Wall acsended. The nomads of the desert were not consumed; civilization was not an oasis. The greetings, "Shalom Aleichem" among Jews and "Salam Aleikem" among Arabs acsended: "Baruch Hashem," and "Inshallah": an imperfect PEACE is ascending in an imperfect world, birthplace of the One and Only Perfect GOD. **The tri-part unity of the Jewish people, the Torah and the Biblical Homeland set a historical precedent.** God's promise of a land flowing with milk and honey is ascending: **"Wherever Jews Go, Grass Grows; Wherever Israelis Go, Gardens Grow."** 13 Nobel Prizes acsended. This year of 5758 is the State of Israel's 50th Anniversary. The Jewish historical past was in the Diaspora; the historical future is in Israel. Some Jews born in Israel live everywhere... on temporary leave. **Israel is the only HOMELAND these Jews will ever know!**

MANY JEWS RECLAIMED GOD

Mathematical and Philosophical Equation for World Peace

WORLD PEACE EQUATION

$$VG + VL = VP$$

Virtue of Good   Value of Life   Vision of Peace

$$VG + VL = VP$$

$$VP = VG + VL$$

$$VP + V(G+L)$$

$$P = (G+L)$$

$$Peace = Good + Life$$

$$Peace = Good\ Life$$

Sharon Esther Lampert

Epilogue

"In all true art, there is vital underlying thought
and artists have accordingly been among the
greatest thinkers of mankind... I even think
that, in the future, art may yet speak, as great poetry
itself with the solemn and majestic ring in which the
Hebrew prophets spoke to the Jews of old, demanding
noble aspirations, condemning the most trenchant
manner vices, and warning us in deep tones against
lapses from morals and duties."

— Rabbi Joseph Herman Hertz

#1 Poetry Website for Student Projects

BE BORN

Be Born.
Become Educated.
Love Your Work.
Make a Meaningful Contribution—
to Yourself, Your Family, and Humanity.
Be a True Friend to Yourself First.
Have Sex with Someone You Love.
Make Love with Complete Abandon.
Enjoy Unconditional Love from Your Devoted Pet.
Make Time to Read the Funnies and Laugh.
Save Enough Money to Visit the Popular,
Pretty, and Peaceful Places of the World.
Read Great Literature, Listen to Great Music,
See Great Art, Watch the Great Movies,
Play the Fun Sports, and Dance till Dawn.
Taste the Great Culinary Delights of the World—
Eat Slowly, Enjoy Every Bite, and Stay in Shape.
Plan One Great Adventure and Stick to the Plan.
Grow Old and Wise.
Leave Your Money to Someone
You Love—Who Loves You Back.
Die in Your Sleep.

—Sharon Esther Lampert

Find the Light and Live in the Light!

#1 Poetry Website for Student Projects

True Love

True Love is Unconditional.
True Love is Found in the Deed.
True Love is Found in the We.
True Love Joins the Heart,
Mind, and Body as One.

By Sharon Esther Lampert

BE ART

ART IS SMART
ART IS OF THE HEART
MAKE ART NOT WAR
YOU ARE BORN FOR GREATNESS
YOR ARE A MASTERPIECE

SHARON ESTHER LAMPERT
www.sharonestherlampert.com

My Metaphysical Life Prophet & Messenger

Part 1. THE 7 COMMANDMENTS
In 2000, I wrote the first "**7 Commandments**," and filed it in a folder.

Part 2. NYC Kabbalah Flyer
In 2000, an ardent fan sent me an online flyer from the NYC Kabbalah Center. The flyer (see below) had a similar format to my **7 Commandments**. I was on my way to a dance class at the 92nd St Y.

Part 3. NYC Kabbalah Flyer
I was too busy to attend the Kabbalah Open House. I kept bumping into the Kabbalah Open House flyer wherever I went that afternoon:
1. Bus Ride: A flyer was sitting next to me on the bus.
2. Sidewalk: There was another flyer on the sidewalk on my way to the dance class. I now had three copies of the flyer, including the one sent by e-mail.

Part 4. Birth of 22 Commandments
It felt as if the flyer was talking to me! I opened the folder that contained my "**7 Commandments**" and read what I had written — and in less than a NY minute, I gave birth to "**The 22 Commandments.**" The miracle of revelation! I am the chosen prophet and messenger!

Part 5. World Famous Poem and Universal Moral Compass for All People
I always read **The 22 Commandments** responsively at open-mic poetry readings (YOUTUBE videos).

One of my ardent fans reads, "**The 22 Commandments**" when visiting his deceased father at the cemetery. I am honored!

"It is not enough to tell people what not to do! It is also important to tell people what to do!"

Sharon Esther Lampert

Princess Kadimah: 8TH Prophetess of Israel

The Kabbalah Flyer, 2002

"Inside every Jewish person is a little Moses trying to get out!"

Chabad Rabbi Ben Tzion Krasnianski

2002

Part 6. Metaphysical Synchronicity

5 minutes after I walked into the Chabad House
for a Shabbat lunch with 50 copies of
"THE 22 COMMANDMENTS,"
to hand out to friends and fans —
the quote cited above is precisely what
Chabad Rabbi Ben Tzion Krasnianski said
right before I handed out the first copy.

What a coincidence!
What an introduction!

My Metaphysical Sister: Hannah Szenes
Two Poets on a Mission

Part 1. My Childhood

In 4th grade, I am cast as Hannah Szenes
in a school play. My mother wrote a note on
the school playbill, "My daughter was
parachuted into Hungary to save the Jewish
people from destruction!"

Part 2. Post-College Years
Parachuted into Hungary, NYC
Writing World Famous Poems

After college, I moved to 82nd Street,
Manhattan, NYC. I was living in the heart of
the NYC Hungarian community. My apartment
was between the Hungarian Cultural Center
and the Hungarian Church. I wrote almost all
of my poetry, philosophy, and education books
in my shoe-box studio apartment.

Part 3. 2004-Present
Hungarian Best Friend & Family

In 2004, I met N.Y.U. Professor Karl Bardosh,
a Hungarian Jew. He became my best friend,
my family, and my MUSE.

Part 4. 2013-Present
The Rescue of Hungarian-
Holocaust Documentation

In Florida, I rescued Hungarian-Holocaust
documentation that had been tucked away
in a drawer for 30 years.

Part 5. Hannah & I Are Bonded for Life

I have a cosmic-spiritual connection to Hannah
Szenes from childhood through adulthood.
I light a beautiful candle to celebrate her
birthday. I light a candle to memorialize her
murder by the NAZIS.

Part 6. Hannah's Poem
"Hora to an Exiled Girl"

Hannah Senezes wrote a poem about
a blue-eyed girl. Did she feel my
presence even before I was born?

Eli, Eli

"My God, My God,
I pray that these
things never end,
The sand and the sea,
The rustle of the waters,
Lightning of the heavens,
The prayer of man!"

Hannah Sezenes
Jewish Hungarian Poet
Israeli War Heroine

July 17, 1921 — November 7, 1944

SHARON ESTHER LAMPERT
V.E.S.S.E.L. Very. **E**xtra. **S**pecial. **S**haron. **E**sther. **L**ampert.

PRODIGY
• 10 Esoteric Laws of Genius and Creativity: Unleash the Creator The God Within

POET — One of The World's Greatest Poets
The Greatest Poems Ever Written on Extraordinary World Events
POETRY WORLD RECORD: "Though The Eyes of Eve"
http://famouspoetsandpoems.com/poets.html

PROPHET — 8TH Prophetess of Israel
GOD TALKS TO ME: A Working Definition of God **GOD IS GO! DO!**
22 COMMANDMENTS: All You Will Ever Need to Know About God

PHILOSOPHER QUEEN
• God of What? 11 Esoteric Laws of Inextricability, Is Life a Gift or a Punishment?
• Temporary Insanity: We Are All Building Our Lives on a **S**and Trap — Written in Letter **S**
• Sperm Manifesto: 10 Rules for the Road
• Women Have All The Power But Have Never Learned How to Use It

PEACEMAKER
World Peace Equation

PIONEER
• Silly Little Boys: 40 Rules of Manhood — For Men of All Ages
• **C**UPID: Language of Love — Written in Letter **C**
• **D**ESTINY: Are You Living Life By **D**efault or By **D**esign? — Written in Letter **D**
• **P**UBLISH: SECRET SAUCE of Book Sales — Written in Letter **P**
• LYMTY: Love You More Than Yesterday — 14 Relationship Strategies for Happily After Ever
• WIN AT THIN: FAT ME, SKINNY ME What Works, What Doesn't
• SEX ON A PLATE: FOOD AS FOREPLAY
• SCHMALTZY: In America, Even a Cat Can Have a Dream, ages 8-12

PALADIN OF EDUCATION – SMARTGRADES BRAIN POWER REVOLUTION
• The Silent Crisis Destroying America's Brightest Minds - BOOK OF THE MONTH
• 40 Universal Gold Standards of Education
• 10 SMARTGRADES Learning Tools: EVERY DAY AN EASY A.com
• 15 Stepping Stones of Academic Success
• 15 Stumbling Blocks of Academic Failure

PHOTON
SUPERHERO OF EDUCATION
www.PhotonSuperhero.com

PERFORMER
Vocalist: Ashira Orchestra (YOUTUBE videos)

PLAYER: JOCK
N.Y.U. Women's Varsity Basketball Team, N.Y.C. Marathon, Skiing, and Tennis

PHOENIX

PINUP
SEXIEST CREATIVE GENIUS IN HUMAN HISTORY

NYU

Honored Sharon Esther Lampert with an **AWARD** for
"Multi-Interdisciplinary Studies" (YOUTUBE videos)

- **Pr**odigy
- **P**oet
- **P**rophet
- **P**hilosopher
- **P**eacemaker
- **P**rincess & **P**ea
- **P**INUP
- **P**erformer: Vocalist
- **P**layer: Jock
- **P**aladin of Education
- **P**HOTON SUPERHERO
- **P**rincess Kadimah
- **P**resident
- **P**ublisher
- **P**roducer
- **P**sychobiologist
- **P**iano-**P**laying Cat
- **P**hoenix

Websites:
- SharonEstherLampert.com
- WorldFamousPoems.com
- PoetryJewels.com
- PhilosopherQueen.com
- Schmaltzy.com
- TrueLoveBurnsEternal.com
- SillyLittleBoys.com
- WinAtThin.com
- WritersRunTheWorld.com
- HappyGrandparenting.com
- BooksArePowerful.com
- GodIsGoDo.com

SMARTGRADES
BRAIN POWER REVOLUTION
- Smartgrades.com
- BooksNotBombs.com
- EverydayanEasyA.com
- PhotonSuperHero.com

Artists March to the Beat of a Different Drummer
Sharon Esther Lampert Marches to the Beat of an Entire Orchestra

Poet, Philosopher, Prophet
Paladin of Education, Peacemaker,
Princess & Pea, Phoenix, PHOTON, PINUP, Prodigy

Big-Blue Eyes.   Brilliant Books.   Beautiful & Buxom.

Sharon Esther Lampert was born an **OLD SOUL** — She was never young! Sharon is a lefty.

The **IDEA** of Sharon Esther was conceived of in **ISRAEL**. Her Holocaust survivor refugee father immigrated to Israel. Her mother vacationed in Israel. They met, married, and Sharon was born.

At age nine, her mother declared: "My daughter is a poet, philosopher, and teacher!" She nicknamed her daughter, "The Princess and the Pea!"

At age 9, Sharon Esther was writing books on memo pads, and binding them together with a stapler.

Her mother would make **5OX** of Sharon's poems on her office copy machine.

Sharon Esther's greatest literary works woke her up in the middle of the night — and made her get up out of bed — and write them down. Sharon writes an entire book in one day or one night! Sharon Esther's books write themselves!

Sharon Esther's literary genius is to commingle poetry, philosophy, and comedy into a single sentence.

Sharon's mother was the sole person in Sharon's life who knew who she was from the **INSIDE OUT!** Her beloved mother also knew to her very last breath... the exact day and to the minute when she would die! (Eve Paikoff Lampert: June 3, 1925 — May 5, 1985).

Sharon Esther's Gifts Are Metaphysical — Beyond the Scope of Scientific Inquiry

There Are No Rough Drafts! — Sharon's Books Write Themselves!
(There Are 4 Books with God in the Title)

"A LIST" Sharon Esther Lampert is One of the World's Greatest Poets
http://famouspoetsandpoems.com/poets.html

#1 Poetry Website for School Projects
On a global scale, Sharon's poetry is used by teachers for their poetry lesson plans, and by students for their poetry school projects.

New York University Awards (YOUTUBE videos)
Sharon Esther earned three degrees from NYU — and she was honored with two NYU awards. Sharon represented her class at her Gallatin graduation — and was honored with an award for **"Multi-Interdisciplinary Studies."** Sharon also played on the NYU Women's Varsity Basketball Team as a Center in the $16-million Coles Sports Center. Sharon won an "NYU Weightlifting Contest" — Sharon was the sole contestant — so she won! (NYU newspaper article).

Fan Mail
Cody Howell H.S. Student

FANS@SharonEstherLampert.com

Cody Howell
1042 Prospect Dr.
Imperial, Mo 63052
May 2, 2005

Sharon Esther Lampert
P.O.BOX 103,
New York, New York,10028,US

Dear, Sharon E. Lampert
Hello, My name in Cody, I am a Junior at Windsor High School in Missouri. I have had the chance to write to any one person and I picked you. I have always enjoyed quotes and sayings. Theirs just something about it, like I have always known there is a "better way" but never really found anything until I started to pay attention that their was more than just physical happenings. The poet has the ability to drink from streams science has yet to discover. I used to always reads one liners like
" a community begins to grow when old men plant trees they know they will never enjoy the shade of." Things like this really interested me. Something more than what I had known.

I am very curious by nature, and this kind of wisdom/intellect really hit the spot for me, now I have many poems, sayings, quotes ext. I can't recite them by heart but I thourouly enjoyed the ones I read. I didn't know of you until me and my buddy were talking about how we like psychology and basically more than average and the "better way". After reading some of your quotes I realized you must have seen your share of happenings and become very wise over the years of thought, poetry, and life.

My first thought was to write to you and try to flatter you because I enjoyed your work. Well I guess you made your poetry your work. Then I started thinking that this well of knowledge , all that stuff you've learned, it would be a long shot but my curiosity wouldn't stop unless if I asked you if you could share some of the knowledge you have gained. Any and all would be appreciated and probably useful later considering I am still just a 17-year-old kid. I can't think of any other word than greedy, but you have already thought so many with your influences, and I ask you to help me out, If your busy you have already done more than enough, thank you, and thanks for your time while reading this. I am sorry but I always find myself looking for more and I'm positive you have gained useful info in your day. I could imagine the child who has heard many stories, lesions, and wisdoms of many. He'd be one of the most diverse ,intelligent humans around, and with something like this in mind how could I not be greedy.

I have already learned some from Internet, friends like the one who told me about poems, and family. I have tried to learn patience from the impatient, kindness from the angry, and truth from fools, but for some reason I'm not thankful for these teachers. I still feel as if I could have more, and the lessons of an older experienced poet just has something about how it sounds. Greatness is all I've seen come from poets their ability to make one think is amazing , I could just imagine the wisdom of an experienced one.

Either way I just wanted to say thank you for your time and thank you for doing what you have done. Your shared wisdom and lessons will help many and your work might not be remembered forever but I believe that your positive effect will. Thank you again

Your student ,
Cody

#1 Poetry Website
For Student Projects

FAN MAIL

POET@WORLDFAMOUSPOEMS.COM

KADIMAH 8TH PROPHETESS OF ISRAEL

Fan Mail
President of My Fan Club
Rabbi David Posner

Congregation Emanu-El
of the City of New York
Fifth Avenue at Sixty-fifth Street
New York, N.Y. 10021-6596

Study of
DAVID M. POSNER

September 22, 1999

The New York Public Library
Humanities and Social Sciences Library
Fifth Avenue and 42nd Street
New York, NY 10018-2788

Dear Friends:

Sharon Esther Lampert has made application for a fellowship from the Center for Scholars and Writers. It is with greatest pleasure that I write to you in support of her application.

I can best describe this remarkable woman by citing the analysis of Moses Maimonides, in his "Guide for the Perplexed," concerning psychological endowments. He noted the class of people who are intellectually superior, but whose imaginative faculties are deficient. These, he said, were philosophers. Then there are those whose imaginative faculties are highly developed, but who are deficient intellectually. He said these are dreamers and politicians. But then he observed the rare people who have both highly developed intellects and imaginations. These, he said, are prophets.

Sharon Esther Lampert falls into the last category. She has one of the most gifted intellects I have ever encountered, and her imaginative capacity is absolutely awesome.

I have known many people throughout my long career at Temple Emanu-El. I have never met anyone like this extraordinary human being.

Again, awesome is the most appropriate word.

Yours truly,

FORMED BY THE CONSOLIDATION OF EMANU-EL CONGREGATION AND TEMPLE BETH-EL

Fan Mail
MOMMY

At Age 9,
MOMMY Knew Who I Was
from the **INSIDE OUT**!

Darling Sharon,
The Queen Has Arrived!
My daughter is a poet, philosopher, and teacher!
My daughter is the **P**rincess & the **P**ea!
Beauty & **B**rains!
MOMMY, XOXO

Sharon Esther Lampert
Sexiest Creative Genius
in Human History
PINUP

FAN MAIL
FANS@SharonEstherLampert.com

A PHENOMENON...
SHARON ESTHER LAMPERT

Lithe and lovely ... like a fawn.
This lady fascinates me ... from dusk till dawn.
Feminine and comely ... she's beyond belief
A blue-beam from her eyes ... is my soothing relief.

Girlish in her braces ... maidenly in her style
I yearn for her embraces ... and adore her friendly smile.
As tasteful as any artist ... you'll ever see
She's a compendium of class ... from A to Z.

If you'd like to see a figure, that puts Venus to shame
Behold her in a swimsuit, and your passions will aflame.
Ever exuding goodness . . . guided from above
Miss Sharon is the essence, and epitome of Love.

She's the inspiration of sages, and also fools like me
And the most magnificent female, I'm sure I'll ever see.
The nights are now endearing, & never filled with doubt
I sometimes wake up singing, cause it's Sharon . . .
I dream about.

Affectionately, . .
A devoted fan,
—Harry McVeety

Dear Sharon,

You are not only an exquisite poet, you're beautiful! Am smitten by your luminous beingness. Are you an angel in disguise--a so-called malachim in Hebrew if I am not mistaken.

Thank you for your wondeful open-hearted response. Your photo will sit next to those of Gautama Buddha and the Blessed Virgin Mary. I will follow your sound esoteric advise regarding the positioning of your photo and the two other icons.

I am deeply impressed that you are very conscious about the concept of sacred space and the flow of spiritual energy. So please send me your precious photo as soon as possible.

P.S. Will you be generous enough to send me your signed photo which I will place on the secret altar of my heart, lit by the menorah, the seven-stemmed candelabra of your inspiration, O mystical muse, O Rose of Sharon...

Your ardent fan and admirer,

— Felix Fojas, the cybercat with a mystical meow

Chico, CA,95926

FANS@SharonEstherLampert.com

December 2001

Dear Kadimah:

You are truly a remarkable woman. You are a wonderful word-weaver.

You are great in spirit and inspire everyone.

You have insights on multiple things. You "see" while others stumble along.

That is why you bear the Light. That is why you cry out for Hope in the midst of despair. That is why you are always a step away from the multitude, yet when you speak they cry,

"She is our voice and says what we have felt all the time."

Blessed are those who have you for a friend.

Sincerely,
—Reverend Aaron R. Orr
Hamilton, Ontario, Canada
http://owensinc.freeyellow.com

WHO AM I?
My Name is Aaron Robin Orr and I was born in Belfast, Northern Ireland on November 16, 1940 the only son of Andrew Orr and Hessie Orr. They were Presbyterian by denomination and Christian by life and practice. In September 1965 I married my wife, the former Ruth Hannah Hawkins and never has a man been more blessed than I. We have two children, Elizabeth and Andrew. Beth is married to our son-in-law Remo Pace, gave us our first granddaughter Rachael almost two years ago. Andrew is still single and is involved in various endeavours one of which is writing for an Internet magazine.

What Happens When You
Dress Up Albert Einstein
As Marilyn Monroe?

Sharon Esther Lampert

One of the World's Greatest Poets

http://famouspoetsandpoems.com/poets.html

Famous Poets and Poems   http://famouspoetsandpoems.com/poets.html

 Larry Levis (3)
(1946 - 1996)

 Amy Levy (69)
(1861 - 1889)

 Louise Labe (1)
(1524 - 1566)

 David Lehman (58)
(1948 - present)

 Jiri Mordecai Langer (1)
(1894 - 1943)

 John Lindley (4)
(1952 - present)

 Dimitris Lyacos (3)
(1966 - present)

 Yahia Lababidi (10)
(1973 - present)

 Laurie Lee (6)
(1914 - 1997)

 Walter Savage Landor (52)
(1775 - 1864)

 Michael Lally (1)
(1942 - present)

 Major Henry Livingston, Jr. (23)
(1748 - 1828)

 Roddy Lumsden (2)
(1966 - present)

 Sharmagne Leland-St. John (5)
(1953 - present)

 Sharon Esther Lampert (19)
(0 - present)

M

 Claude McKay (76)
(1889 - 1948)

 Spike Milligan (35)
(1918 - 2002)

 Marianne Moore (18)
(1887 - 1972)

 John Milton (102)
(1608 - 1674)

 A. A. Milne (22)
(1882 - 1956)

 Czeslaw Milosz (33)
(1911 - 2004)

 Edgar Lee Masters (251)
(1868 - 1950)

 William Matthews (10)
(1942 - 1997)

 Edwin Muir (14)
(1887 - 1959)

 Roger McGough (14)
(1937 - present)

 Walter de la Mare (44)
(1873 - 1956)

 Antonio Machado (8)
(1875 - 1939)

 Edna St. Vincent Millay (165)
(1892 - 1950)

 W. S. Merwin (23)
(1927 - present)

 John Masefield (25)
(1878 - 1967)

 Louis MacNeice (3)
(1907 - 1963)

 Thomas Moore (144)
(1779 - 1852)

 Christopher Marlowe (6)
(1564 - 1593)

KADIMAH PRESS: GIFTS of GENIUS

Revelations! My Books Write Themselves!

18 Books of Poetry
Poet: The Greatest Poems Ever Written on Extraordinary World Events
Title: I Stole All the Words from the Dictionary
#1 Poetry Website for School Projects
A List: One of the World's Greatest Poets
ISBN Hardcover: 978-1-885872-06-7
ISBN Paperback: 978-1-885872-07-4
ISBN E-Book: 978-1-885872-08-1

25 Books
EDUCATION

Prodigy:WORLD PREMIERE!
Title: Unleash the Creator The God Within
10 Esoteric Laws of Genius and Creativity
ISBN Hardcover: 978-1-885872-21-0
ISBN Paperback: 978-1-885872-22-7
ISBN E-Book: 978-1-885872-23-4

Prophet:WORLD PREMIERE! **GOD IS GO! DO!**
Title: GOD TALKS TO ME: A WORKING DEFINITION OF GOD
ISBN Hardcover: 978-1-885872-33-3
ISBN Paperback: 978-1-885872-34-0
ISBN E-Book: 978-1-885872-36-4

Prophet:WORLD PREMIERE!
Title: The 22 Commandments: All You Will Ever Need to Know About God
A Universal Moral Compass For All People, For All Religions, For All Time
ISBN Hardcover: 978-1-885872-03-6
ISBN Paperback: 978-1-885872-04-3
ISBN E-Book: 978-1-885872-05-0

Philosopher:WORLD PREMIERE!
Title: God of What? 11 Esoteric Laws of Inextricability
Is Life a Gift or a Punishment? 11 Absolute Truths
ISBN Hardcover: 978-1-885872-00-5
ISBN Paperback: 978-1-885872-01-2
ISBN E-Book: 978-1-885872-02-9

All Global Bookstores

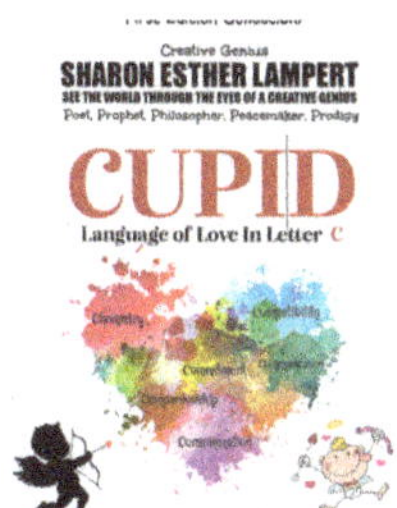

Prodigy: **WORLD PREMIERE!**
Title: **CUPID: Language of Love — Written in Letter C**
ISBN Hardcover: 978-1-885872-55-5
ISBN Paperback: 978-1-885872-56-2
ISBN E-Book: 978-1-885872-57-9
SharonEstherLampert.com

Prodigy: **WORLD PREMIERE!**
Title: **TEMPORARY INSANITY**
We Are All Building Our Lives on a Sand Trap- Written in Letter S
ISBN Hardcover: 978-1-885872-70-8
ISBN E-Book: 978-1-885872-71-5
SharonEstherLampert.com

Popular: **Children's Book, Ages 8-12**
Title: **SCHMALTZY: IN AMERICA, EVEN A CAT CAN HAVE A DREAM**
ISBN Hardcover: 978-1-885872-39-5
ISBN Paperback: 978-1-885872-38-8
ISBN E-Book: 978-1-885872-37-1
Schmaltzy.com

Color-Coded
Vocabulary Words

Popular: **WORLD PREMIERE**
Title: **SILLY LITTLE BOYS: 40 RULES OF MANHOOD**
HOW DO SILLY LITTLE BOYS GROW INTO SANE BIG MEN
14 Global Catastrophes of Violence Against Women
ISBN Hardcover: 978-1-885872-29-6
ISBN Paperback: 978-1-885872-35-7
ISBN E-Book: 978-1-885872-41-8
SillyLittleBoys.com

Popular: **Every Relationship Begins with a Great Meal**
Title: **SEX ON A PLATE: FOOD AS FOREPLAY**
THE COOKBOOK OF EVERLASTING LOVE
ISBN Hardcover: 978-1-885872-46-3
ISBN Paperback: 978-1-885872-48-7
ISBN E-Book: 978-1-885872-47-0
TrueLoveBurnsEternal.com

THANK YOU

Count Your Blessings. Practice Gratitude

"Never Underestimate the Power of a Girl with a Book"
—ICON Supreme-Court Justice Ruth Bader Ginsburg

1. My Gifts — Genetic Inheritance of Genius:
- Lefty: Born with an Extra Body Part: "Creative Apparatus"
- Two Sets of Artsy-Fartsy Genes: Painter Maternal Grandfather Benjamin Paikoff and Sculptor Father Abraham Lampert
- Vocalist: Ashira Orchestra (YOUTUBE videos)
- Athlete: NYU Women's Varsity Basketball Team

2. My Life: Dawn of Digital Revolution:
- APPLE: The Golden Age of Personal Computers
- ADOBE: The Golden Age of Creativity
- INGRAM: The Golden Age of POD
- SOCIAL MEDIA: The Golden Age Internet & Globalization

3. My Loved Ones:
- SELFLOVE: Mindfulness, Mantra, and Music Mitigates **MADNESS!**
- My MOMMY: Unconditional True Love
- My PURRfect Children: SCHMALTZY & FALAFEL, Schmaltzy.com (YOUTUBE videos)
- My Muse Karl Bardosh "Friends First and Forever and Family"
- My Metaphysical Sister: Poet Hannah Sezenes: "ELI, ELI"
- My 7 Practice Husbands, Artist & Muses, Dates and NYC Nightlife

4. My Education: NYU BA, MA, and MA and Awards (YOUTUBE videos)
- NYU Professor Laurin Raiken: NYU **"Multi-Interdisciplinary Award"** and M.A. **Class Representative at Graduation**
- ROCKEFELLER UNIVERSITY, NYC, Publication: "Hyperphagia and Obesity Induced by Neuropeptide Y"
- **AWARD:** 100-Year Scholarship Award Winner, By NYC Mayor Edward Koch
- **AWARD:** Empire Science Scholarship Award Winner
- **AWARD:** First Prize: Upper East Side Resident Writing Contest
- **AWARD:** Jerusalem Fellowship Award of Aish Hatorah, Israel
- Won a NYU Weightlifting Contest, NYU Coles Sports Center (article in NYU Washington Square News)

5. My Sports:
- NYC Marathon
- Basketball: NYU Women's Varsity Basketball Team, Center
- Basketball: NYC Urban Professional League, Center and Guard
- Skiing: Heavenly, Lake Tahoe, Nevada
- Tennis: Central Park NYC Tennis Courts
- Basketball and Baseball: Coach Sandy Pyonin
- Baseball: Coaches Hall of Fame Jean Harding and Wilma Briggs
- Basketball Coaches: Chicago Phil Jackson and Bill Walton

6. My Inspirations:
- ISRAEL: "AM YISRAEL CHAI!" Sheep to Slaughter to Light of the World — Less Than 1% of Population & 22% of 5 Nobel Prizes
- Rabbi David Posner, NYC Temple Emanu-El, "President of My Fan Club"
- NYC: The Golden Age of Personal Freedom & Creative Self-Expression

NYU President Andrew Hamilton and Me

NYU Special Mention

NYU President John Brademas (backed his limosine into my bicycle)
Professor Yael Feldman (the writer's relationship to MOMMY)
Professor Paul Humphreys (family therapy class)
Professor Ted Coons, (my position at Rockefeller University)
John, The Security Guard at Coles Sports Center (SUPERFAN)
NYU B-Ball Coaches: Evelyn Hannon and Sherri Pickard

NYU Professor Karl Bardosh and Me

NYU Professor Laurin Raiken and Me

South Florida Sun-Sentinel

DELRAY BEACH NEWS   PALM BEACH COUNTY NEWS

Spirituality workshop supports A Walk on Water fund

MARCI SHATZMAN MSHATZMAN@TRIBPUB.COM | JAN 20, 2016

Sharon Esther Lampert didn't bring her tiara when she moved here from New York, but she found one just in time to be one of the speakers at Barbara M. Wolk's second annual Spirituality Workshop Jan. 24.

"Barbara has this wonderful event in support of autistic children," said Lampert, an author, poet, philosopher and educator who plays a princess for her talks.

She expects to hand out her "30 Commandments: All You Ever Need to Know," at the workshop from 10:30 a.m. to 12:30 p.m. at the Shirley & Barton Weisman Community Center, 7091 W. Atlantic Ave., in Delray Beach.

Admission is a minimum of $10 and the event opens at 10 a.m. A live auction will include a sculpture called "Balance."

I Am Mortal.
My Books Are Immortal.
Please Handle My Books Gently.
My Books Are My Remains.

This book was compiled in 5 parts:
Part 1. Birth of 7 Commandments, 2000 (I filed it!)
Part 2. Birth of 22 Commandments, 2000 (metaphysical)
Part 3. Poetry Readings at Barnes & Noble: 2002-Present
          (YOUTUBE videos)
Part 4. Essays, June 1-2, 2022 (20 Years Later)
Part 5. Published, August 2022 (20 Years Later)

Sharon Esther Lampert

SEE THE WORLD THROUGH THE EYES OF A CREATIVE GENIUS
Prophet, Poet, Philosopher, Peacemaker, Paladin of Education, PHOTON SUPERHERO, Prodigy

EDUCATION FAIR USE NOTICE